Written by Sophie Edgar

Illustrated by Loren Grosvenor

For Sophie's amazing step-daughter, Lucy, who is no longer afraid of bees.
Also, for Dave, the original Mr Bumble, who inspired us to create this book.
#davethebumblebee

Lucy was terrified of bees.
She'd been stung by one when she was little and it had really hurt.

It had stopped her wearing brightly coloured clothes.

Her mum had stopped planting flowers in the garden to try and make the bees stay away.

In the summer, she wouldn't go to the park with her friends any more, just in case there were any bees there.
Lucy thought bees were bad.

One morning, the sun was shining and all of Lucy's friends were going to the park for a picnic. Lucy watched sadly from her bedroom window as her friends ran down the road together. She wished she could go with them but she was just too afraid of being stung by a bee.

Suddenly, something hit the window, making Lucy jump backwards. What was it? She slowly crept back towards the glass and peeped out from behind the window frame. There, on the ledge, was a big bumblebee...

It wasn't moving.

Lucy shut her curtains and hoped the next gust of wind would blow the bee away.

She sat with her back to the window, determined not to look out again. But then she heard a faint tapping sound.

Nervously, Lucy leant closer to the window and opened the curtains just a little.

The bee moved one frail wing as though it was trying to fly but couldn't. Lucy turned away.

She waited a few seconds and then peeped to see if it was still there...

...It was!

The bee hadn't moved but it was looking at her. Its big eyes stared straight at her as if it was pleading for help. She opened the window just a little and the bee crawled inside.

Lucy froze. She didn't know what to do. She had never been this close to a bee before without being stung.

The bee looked too tired to fly, so maybe if she stayed far enough away from it she wouldn't get hurt. Very quietly, she tiptoed backwards towards her bedroom door.

On Lucy's windowsill was a handkerchief. It had belonged to her great grandma and had a little purple flower sewn onto the corner.

The bee crept onto the handkerchief and went to sleep. What was Lucy going to do now?

She needed to find a way to get the bee flying again and out of her bedroom. Maybe she could look on the internet and find out how to look after a bee.

She turned on her tablet and started to make some notes.

Let nature take its course? That sounded like if the bee couldn't fly Lucy would have to put it outside to die. She couldn't do that!

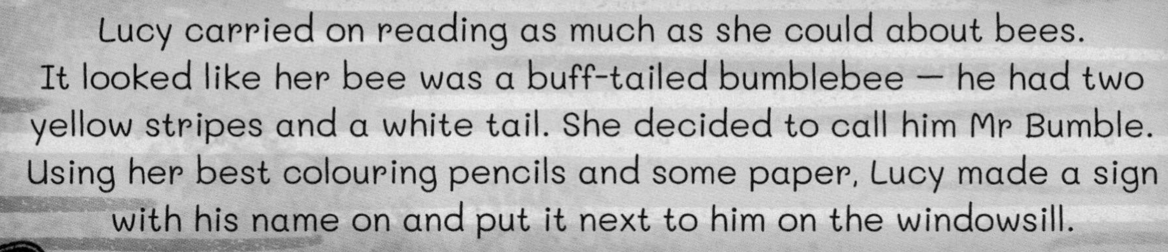

Lucy carried on reading as much as she could about bees. It looked like her bee was a buff-tailed bumblebee — he had two yellow stripes and a white tail. She decided to call him Mr Bumble. Using her best colouring pencils and some paper, Lucy made a sign with his name on and put it next to him on the windowsill.

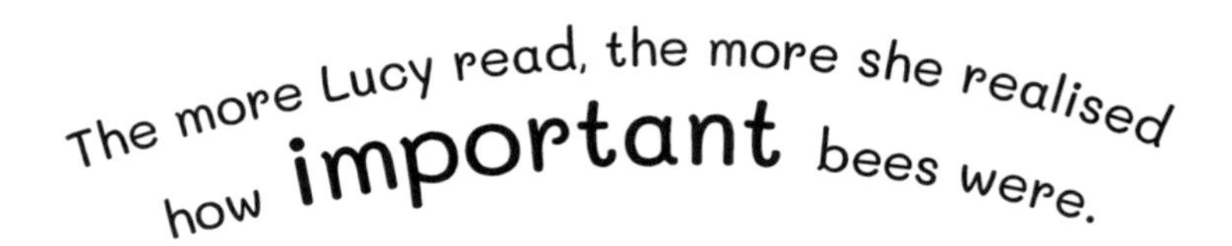

She'd always thought they just made honey, but it turned out that bees did so much more than that!

Every time a bee lands on a flower, it drinks and collects the nectar, but it also collects a special golden dust called pollen. Then when it flies to another flower it leaves some of the pollen there.

This is called pollination and it helps seeds to grow. Fruit and other plants grow from the seeds.

Lucy thought about all the food she liked to eat that she now knew grew with the help of bees: apples, strawberries, blueberries, cucumbers, cherries, melons and so much more.

It wasn't just fruit and vegetables though — bees also helped plants to grow that fed animals. Chickens, sheep, cows, horses — they all needed bees too!

Lucy simply had to **save this bumblebee.**

She thought she saw him shiver and wondered if he was cold.
Looking around her room, she spotted a stripy sock on the floor.
Socks were the only colourful item of clothing she wore.
Everything else in her wardrobe was black or grey.

Carefully, she picked up the sock and placed it next to Mr Bumble. Using all his strength, he crawled inside it and snuggled down.

Lucy thought she saw him smile at her before his antennae flopped over his eyes and he fell into a deep sleep. She laid down on her bed and watched him sleep. He didn't look scary at all.

Tomorrow, she would help him get stronger and learn to fly again.

The next morning, Lucy woke to the sound of buzzing. She leapt out of bed ready to run from the room. Was she having a nightmare?
Then she remembered...

"Mr Bumble!"

Where was he?

She followed the buzzing sound and realised it was coming from under her bed. Lucy bent down and found him nestled between her old teddies and her wooden memory box.

"Did you try to fly?" Lucy asked. She wasn't sure, but she thought she saw Mr Bumble nod. "Maybe you should get your strength up first," she suggested.

Lucy gave him another spoonful of sugar water and left him under her bed

"I know exactly what to do!"

Lucy suddenly shouted, making Mr Bumble jump and fall headfirst into his spoon of sugar water.

Lucy raced from the room and returned a minute later with a small box.

"We have to strengthen your legs and your wings to help you fly again," she explained.

Inside the box were some small twigs and wooden lollipop sticks. First, she gave the twig to Mr Bumble.

"My dad has weights in our garage. He lifts them up over his head to make his arms stronger. Maybe you could try?"

Mr Bumble looked at the twig and prodded it with his front leg.

He buzzed loudly as though he was using all his strength to try and move it. Lucy smiled.

"Don't worry, we'll practise," she said.

Next she placed the lollipop stick on the top of the box. "Climb up on here. You can jump off the end and practise flying," Lucy explained.

Mr Bumble didn't look convinced, but he did as she had suggested and sat nervously on one end of the wooden stick.

"Ready?" Lucy shouted. Mr Bumble nodded. **"Fly!"**

The bumblebee jumped. His four wings flapped furiously, but it was no use — he somersaulted and landed upside down on Lucy's foot.

Normally, having a bee on her foot would have made Lucy scream, but she stayed very calm and let Mr Bumble climb off safely.

Over the next few days, Lucy spent every moment she could helping Mr Bumble fly. She made launchpads out of anything she could find.

She persuaded her mum to buy flowers for the garden and snuck some into her bedroom so that Mr Bumble had nectar to drink.

Every night, he slept on the handkerchief under her bed, inside the stripy sock.

Eventually, Mr Bumble was strong enough to fly around Lucy's room. It was time to let him go back outside. Lucy had grown very attached to her fuzzy little friend.

She didn't want to say goodbye. Carefully, Lucy carried Mr Bumble on his handkerchief and placed him on the windowsill.

"It's time for you to go back outside now, Mr Bumble. You have a very important job to do." Mr Bumble buzzed in agreement, but he looked sad too.

"You have to go to as many flowers as you can to keep spreading the pollen. I know you can do it — you're so strong now!"

Lucy picked up the handkerchief from the window ledge. A silent tear rolled down her cheek.

"Bye bye, Mr Bumble. Thank you for not stinging me," Lucy whispered. "Maybe you could come back and visit me one day."

Mr Bumble looked up at Lucy. She was sure he nodded his head, then off he flew.

Lucy held the handkerchief tightly in her hand and turned around to look at her bedroom. It wasn't as dull as before. She had a vase of flowers on her bookshelf. She'd drawn pictures of flowers and bees to decorate her walls. She hadn't liked her bedroom much before, but now it made her smile.

Every morning when Lucy woke up, she ran to her window to see if Mr Bumble was there.

Lucy and her mum planted poppies, snapdragons and lavender in their front garden to try to attract more bees, but none had appeared.

Lucy tried everything she could. She even added more colour to her room to see if Mr Bumble would come back. She knew bumblebees only lived for a few weeks, so it was unlikely she would see Mr Bumble again.

Lucy closed her new sunflower-patterned curtains and sat on her bed. She was about to give up hope.

Then all of a sudden...

...There was a faint tap on the window, followed by a buzzing sound.

Could it be?

Lucy ran to the window. Outside, buzzing around in circles, was Mr Bumble! But he wasn't alone — on the window ledge sat three other bees, all looking exhausted.

Lucy opened the window and Mr Bumble flew inside. She knew it was him because he flew straight to his handkerchief and sat buzzing as if he was trying to tell her something.

The other three bees slowly crawled inside and sat on the windowsill.

Mr Bumble wanted Lucy to help his friends. He'd brought them to her because she had helped him get better and fly again, and now she could do the same for the other bees.

The girl who was afraid of bees was now the girl who was going to save them!

Lucy got to work straightaway. In just a day, she had transformed her bedroom into a bee rescue centre. She made little areas for them to rest and relax...

...And an area to build their strength back up. As the bees needed to drink, she set up Mr Bumble's Beestro, which served sugar water by the teaspoon and nectar fresh from a flower.

As soon as the bees were ready, she would release them back outside.

Lucy's mum and dad planted more and more flowers in her garden and for the first time since she had been stung, Lucy wore colourful clothes and went to the park with her friends.

A bee landed on her shoulder, but she didn't scream or run away. She sat very still and watched as it realised she wasn't a flower and flew off.

Mr Bumble came back every day with more bees for her to help. She noticed that each time he returned, he looked a bit older and had to rest for longer before he left again.

Then one day, he didn't appear. It was one of his friends instead.

Lucy knew what that meant. She hoped that Mr Bumble had found a beautiful flower to go to for his final drink of nectar. It made her feel very sad inside, but Lucy now knew that

bees were brilliant.

It was her job to make sure everyone else knew that too.

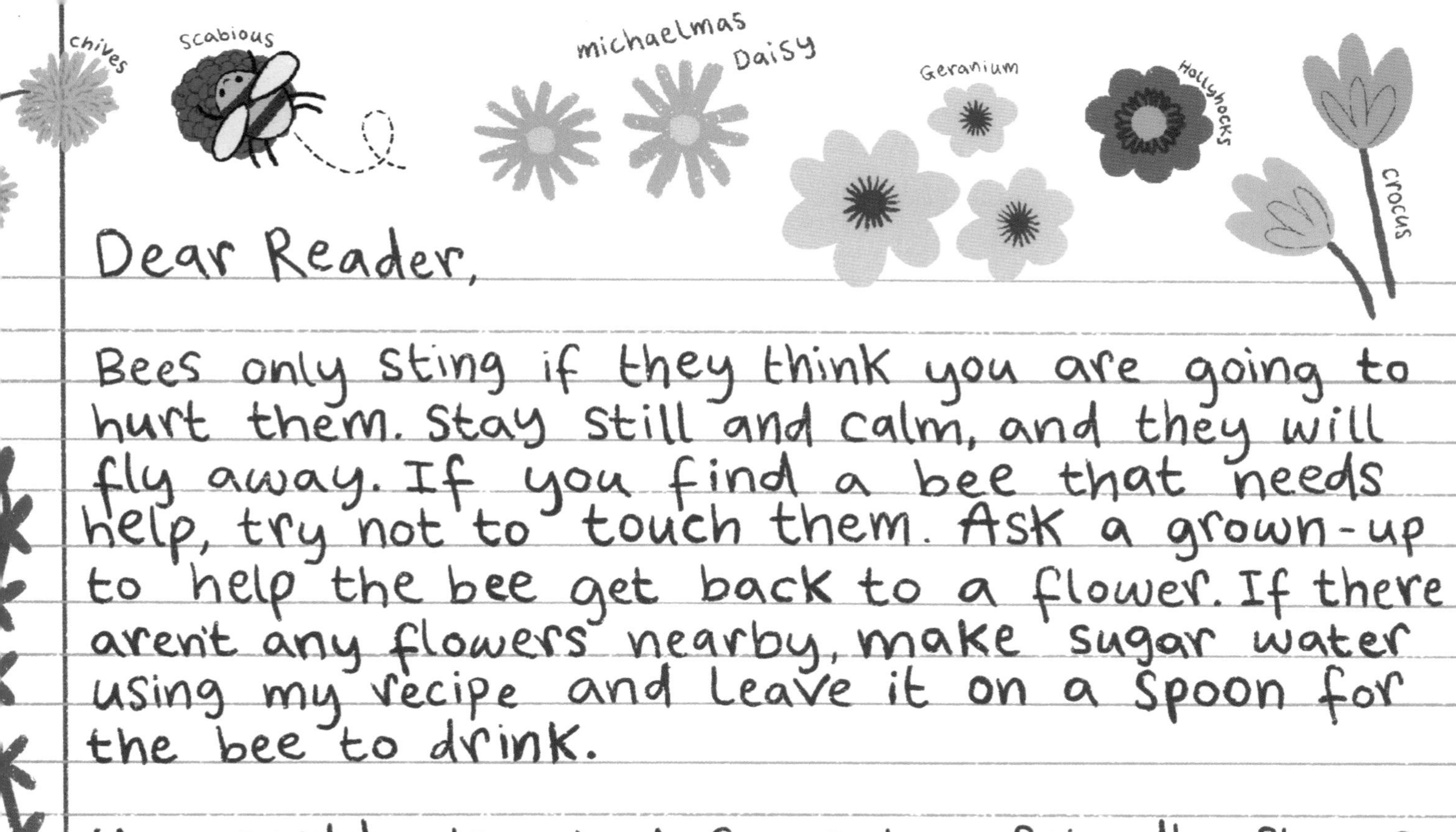

Dear Reader,

Bees only sting if they think you are going to hurt them. Stay still and calm, and they will fly away. If you find a bee that needs help, try not to touch them. Ask a grown-up to help the bee get back to a flower. If there aren't any flowers nearby, make sugar water using my recipe and leave it on a spoon for the bee to drink.

You could also plant some bee-friendly flowers in your garden. There are some examples on this page. You will then have helped to save our bees so they can keep helping our food to grow.

Love from Lucy x

An important message from the Author and Illustrator.

This story is based on a true event. However, if you find a bee in need Always ask a grown-up for help and Never invite bees into your home, especially your bedroom - That part of the story is from our imaginations. Bees belong outside.

Love from Sophie and Loren
xx

About the Author

Sophie Edgar is a mum to three children and has to admit to chasing away a few bees in the past. When she became friends with Loren (illustrator), she realised how important bees are and the more she read about them, the more she wanted to help them.

Now, she spends her time reading, writing and looking after her children and her dog, Teddy, who still chases bees sometimes, but never hurts them. Sophie was a teacher for 15 years and hopes that this book and others in the *Our Mini-beast Heroes* series, will persuade children to look after these creatures when they learn how vital they are to our planet.

You can find out more about Sophie at:

www.sophieedgarauthor.co.uk

Sophie Edgar Author

sophieedgar.author

@SophEdgarAuthor

About the Illustrator

Loren Grosvenor has been illustrating since she was a child and has been drawing and designing professionally for seven years. Her two biggest achievements are graduating with a 1st class honours degree in graphic design and having *Disney* pick one of her hand-lettered designs to use on their homeware and gift wrap.

Loren loves animals and if she can save them, she will. In summer 2020 she found Dave, a buff-tailed bumblebee, who was unable to fly. Loren looked after Dave for five weeks. He was a much-loved addition to the zoo that Loren calls home. Her other pets include her Labrador, Poppy, a falcon called Sid and seven dwarf hamsters.

To find out more about Loren and Dave visit:

www.bluekiwidesign.co.uk

dave_the_bumble_bee & @blue.kiwi.design

When Mr Bumble Came to Stay is the first book in the **Our Mini-beast Heroes** series.

When Mr Bumble Came To Stay

By Sophie Edgar

Illustrated by Loren Grosvenor

First published in 2021 by TeddyPops Publishing

Text copyright © Sophie Edgar 2021
Illustrations copyright
© Loren Grosvenor 2021

All rights reserved.
ISBN: 978-1-9993789-0-5

The rights of the author and illustrator have been asserted in accordance with Sections 77 and 78 of the Copyright Designs and Patents Act, 1988.

No part of this book or its illustrations may be reproduced (including photocopying or storing in any medium by electronic means and whether or not transiently or incidentally to some other use of this publication) without the written permission of the copyright holder except in accordance with the provisions of the Copyright, Design and Patents Act 1988.

Printed in Great Britain
by Amazon

63331545R00020